Idea #9,115
SPACE STATION

Remote manipulator (robotic arm)

Solar charging panels

Cupola (observation area)

Laboratory module

Research module

MAD SCIENTIST
ACADEMY

Zzzzzzz...

THE SPACE DISASTER

MATTHEW McELLIGOTT

CROWN BOOKS
FOR YOUNG READERS
NEW YORK

**To Christy, without whom none
of this would be possible.**

ACKNOWLEDGMENTS
Special thanks to Bob Berman, astronomer and author of terrific
space books, for his stellar advice and galactic guidance.

Copyright © 2017 by Matthew McElligott

All rights reserved. Published in the United States by Crown Books for Young Readers,
an imprint of Random House Children's Books,
a division of Penguin Random House LLC, New York.

Crown and the colophon are registered trademarks of Penguin Random House LLC.

Visit us on the Web! randomhousekids.com

Educators and librarians, for a variety of teaching tools,
visit us at RHTeachersLibrarians.com

Library of Congress Cataloging-in-Publication Data is available upon request.
ISBN 978-0-553-52382-9 (trade)—ISBN 978-0-553-52383-6 (lib. bdg.)—ISBN 978-0-553-52384-3 (ebook)

The text of this book is set in Sunshine.
The illustrations were created with ink, pencil, and digital techniques.

MANUFACTURED IN CHINA
10 9 8 7 6 5 4 3 2 1
First Edition

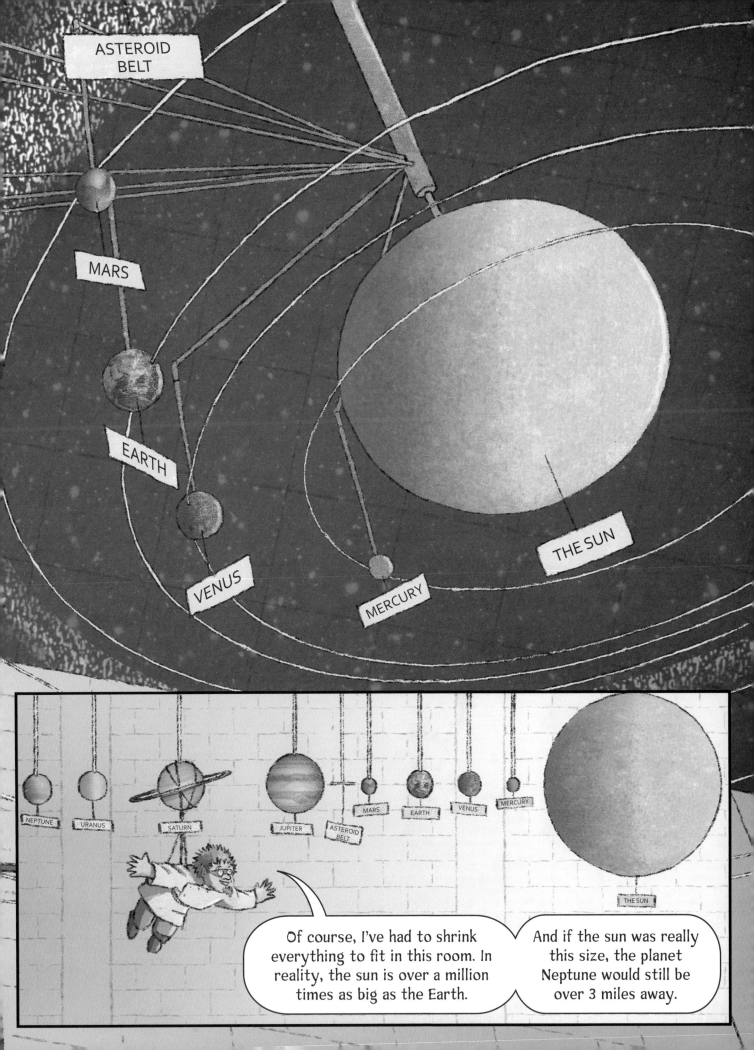

I built this because today we're going to learn all about—

Dr. Cosmic? Are you there, Dr. Cosmic?

Oh, hello, Commander! I'm up here.

Ah, yes. Now I see you.

Students, this is Commander Nova. He's an astronomer.

Good morning, students!

What's an astronomer?

An astronomer is a scientist who studies the stars, planets, moons, and other objects in space.

Tell them where you are.

Right now I'm 250 miles above the Earth in the Mad Scientist Academy Space Station.

Wow!

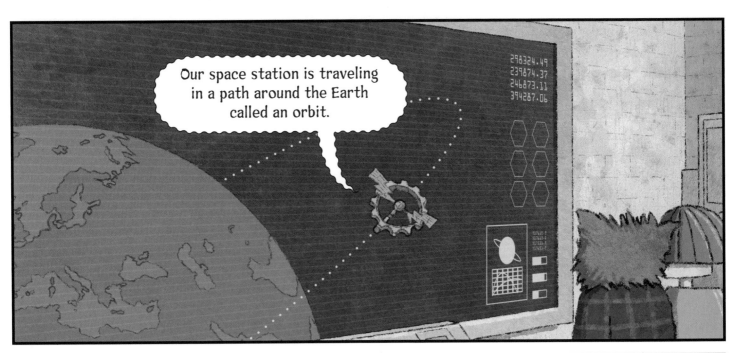

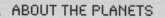
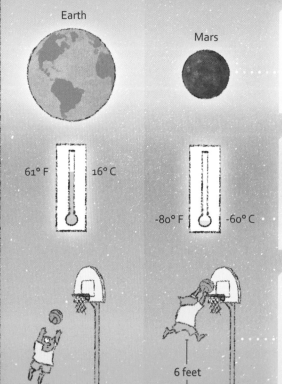

The computer must have started the first challenge. Is this another planet?

If it's a planet, where's the ground?

The handbook says that some planets are made almost entirely of gas.

Maybe that not rainbow. That Saturn's rings!

WHAT ARE THE GAS GIANT PLANETS?

The four largest planets are mostly made of gases. They are all many times larger than Earth.

Relative size of Earth

JUPITER

Jupiter is the largest planet, bigger than the other seven planets combined.

SATURN

Saturn has the most rings of any planet. They are made of ice and dust and are 170,000 miles (273,588 km) across but only about 30 feet (9 m) thick.

URANUS AND NEPTUNE

These planets are also known as the ice giants because they are partially made of layers of ice.

That no moon. That Jupiter! See red spot?

Good thinking, Ken. But then where are we?

WHAT IS A MOON?

A moon is a natural object that orbits around a planet. All planets except Mercury and Venus have at least one moon. Jupiter and Saturn have more than sixty moons each.

PLANETS AND THEIR MOONS

Mecury (0)   Venus (0)   Earth (1)   Mars (2)   Jupiter (67)   Saturn (62)   Uranus (27)   Neptune (14)

The Largest Moons of Jupiter

Io

Europa

Ganymede

Callisto

Jupiter has at least 67 moons, with four very large moons. Three are covered in ice. Scientists think that under the ice on Europa and Ganymede there are huge liquid oceans. They may even contain life.

We must be on one of Jupiter's moons.

Where's the computer? Let's type it in.

I see it! Over here!

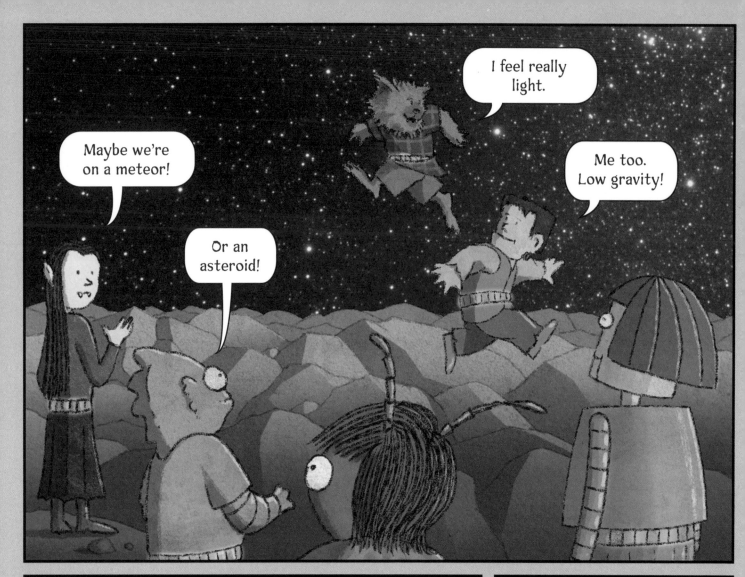

WHAT ARE SPACE ROCKS?

All space rocks orbit the sun. They have very low gravity since they are much smaller than a planet. There are three kinds of space rocks:

ASTEROID

An asteroid is made of rock and sometimes metal. Most asteroids are found in the Asteroid Belt, which is located between Mars and Jupiter.

Asteroids are larger than 33 feet (10 m). The largest known asteroid is 600 miles (950 km) across.

METEOROID

A meteoroid is also made of rock and sometimes metal. If a meteoroid is pulled into Earth's atmosphere by gravity, it is called a meteor, or shooting star. If a meteor doesn't burn up completely before landing on Earth, it is called a meteorite.

Meteoroids are smaller than 33 feet (10 m). They can be as small as specks of dust.

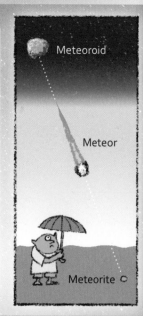

Meteoroid

Meteor

Meteorite

COMET

A comet is made of ice, rock, gas, and dust. When a comet's orbit takes it near the sun, heat can cause ice on the comet to change directly into gas and erupt like a geyser. The gas and dust from these eruptions form the comet's tail.

Comets come in a variety of sizes. They average about 6 miles (10 km) across, not including the tail.

Tail

Explosions

THE SOLAR SYSTEM

SUN

864,938 MILES (1,392,684 KM) ACROSS.
ABOUT ONE MILLION EARTHS COULD FIT
INSIDE THE SUN.

MERCURY

3,031 MILES (4,879 KM) ACROSS.
MERCURY IS THE SMALLEST PLANET, ONLY
A LITTLE BIGGER THAN EARTH'S MOON.
ITS SURFACE IS AS DARK AS BLACK PAINT.

VENUS

7,521 MILES (12,104 KM) ACROSS.
THE GREENHOUSE GASES MAKE VENUS THE
HOTTEST PLANET AT 863° F (462° C), EVEN
HOTTER THAN MERCURY. ITS SURFACE IS AS
WHITE AND SHINY AS SNOW.

EARTH

7,926 MILES (12,756 KM) ACROSS.
EARTH IS THE ONLY PLANET KNOWN TO
HAVE LIFE. MOST OF THE PLANET IS
COVERED IN LIQUID WATER.

MARS

4,220 MILES (6,792 KM) ACROSS.
MARS HAS THE TALLEST MOUNTAIN IN THE
SOLAR SYSTEM. IT IS OVER TWICE AS TALL
AS THE TALLEST MOUNTAIN ON EARTH.

JUPITER

88,846 MILES (142,984 KM) ACROSS.
JUPITER'S GIANT RED SPOT IS A STORM
THAT IS BIGGER THAN THE EARTH.

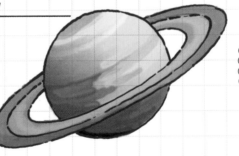

(RED SPOT)

SATURN

74,897 MILES (120,536 KM) ACROSS.
THIS PLANET ROTATES VERY QUICKLY.
A DAY ON SATURN IS ONLY 10 HOURS
AND 34 MINUTES LONG.

For more space facts,
links, projects, and games,
be sure to visit

madscientistacademybooks.com

URANUS

31,763 MILES (51,118 KM) ACROSS.
URANUS HAS THE COLDEST
TEMPERATURES, WITH A LOW
OF −371° F (−224° C).

NEPTUNE

30,775 MILES (49,528 KM) ACROSS.
WINDS ON NEPTUNE ARE EXTREMELY FAST,
SOMETIMES OVER 1,000 MILES PER HOUR.

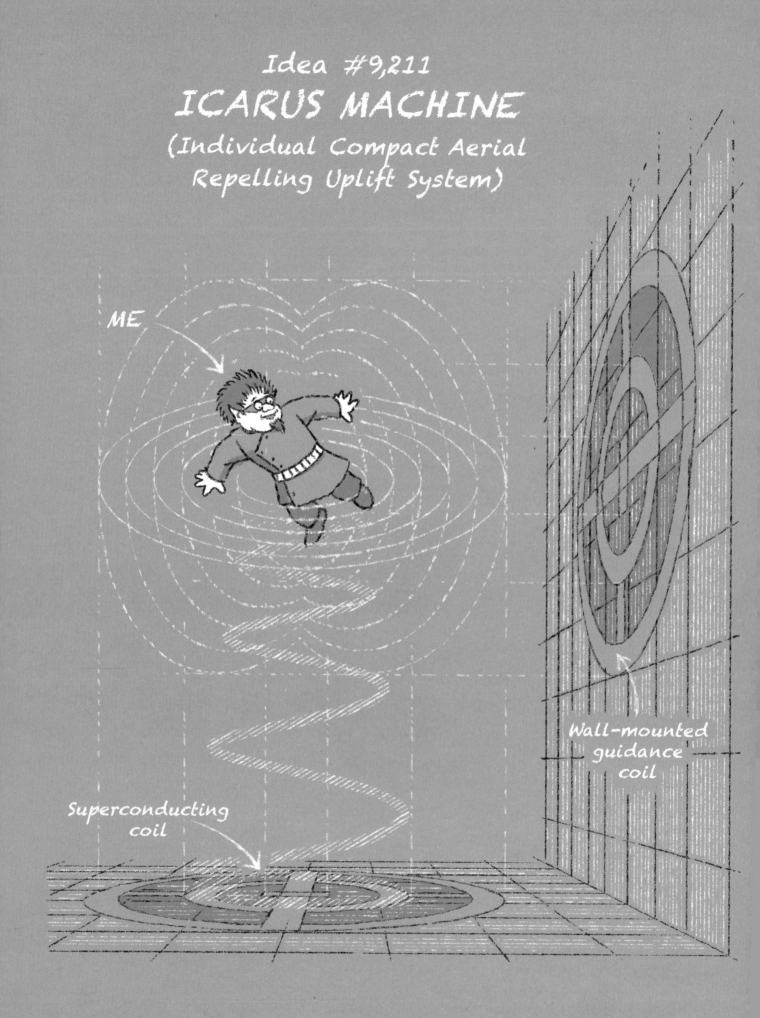